thirteen O'clock

For M.L.S.

Book design by James Stimson.
Typeset in Times New Roman. The illustrations in this book were rendered in pencil.
Manufactured in Hong Kong.

Library of Congress Cataloging-in-Publication Data
Stimson, James.
Thirteen O'clock / by James Stimson.
p. cm.
Summary: As a mysterious old clock strikes thirteen, monsters and ghouls appear looking for a snack
and a little mischief at the expense of the small girl who lives down the hall. .
ISBN 0-8118-4839-6
[1. Monsters—Fiction. 2. Clocks and watches—Fiction. 3.Tricks—Fiction.] I. Title.
PZ7.S86014Th 2005
[Fic]—dc22
2004020719

Distributed in Canada by Raincoast Books, 9050 Shaughnessy Street, Vancouver, British Columbia V6P 6E5

10 9 8 7 6 5 4 3 2 1

Chronicle Books LLC, 85 Second Street, San Francisco, California 94105

www.chroniclekids.com

James Stimson

Thirteen O'clock

chronicle books · san francisco

It was the middle of the late hours,
twelve fifty-nine to be precise.
The winds howled outside,
and the old house creaked–

the small girl thought it all quite nice! It was a fairly normal night, in a *fairly* normal house, that is with the exception of one thing—

this old house had an old clock whose numbers counted not twelve...

... but a spooky number **thirteen** .

Tick Tock,
Tock tick,
Tick tock tick ...

GONG

Atop the mysterious old clock
a hidden hatch flipped.
And upon the freaky 1st of thirteen o'clock's tones,
from it sprang a spriteful FRIGHT
who would have seemed more at home
with his name on a tombstone
than clickity clacking about at night.

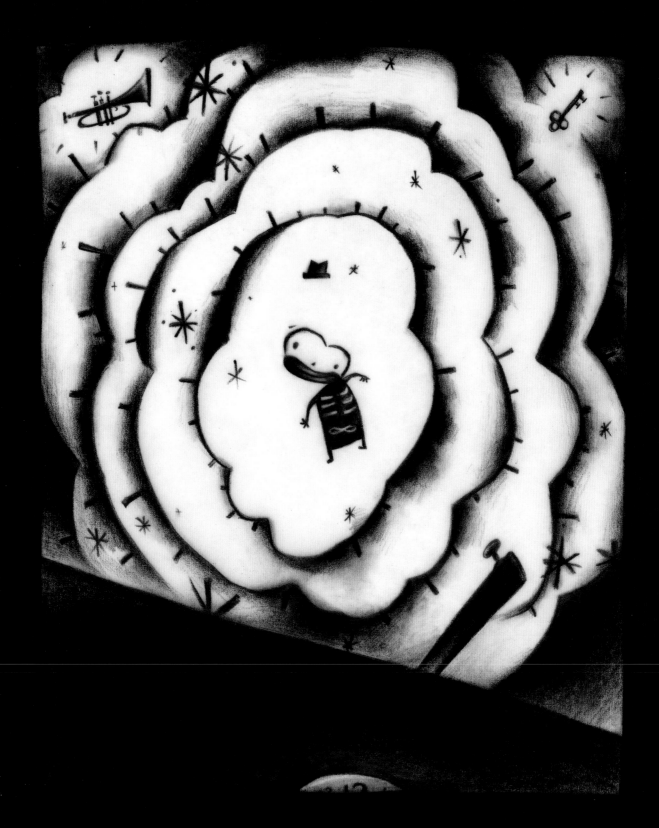

Knock Knock Shake Rattle & Rock,
the 2nd bell of thirteen o'clock binged!
The skeleton with a skeleton key
unlocked the odd clock's *small* door
to free his monsterous friend

the THING

Now, Thing may seem a *strange* name,
but it's really not at all when the thing is explained.
For a thing on its own, may be something unknown—
but known or not it is still a thing!

What is it? What is it? What makes the odd timer *tick*??
What's that inside that swings and sways ??
Is it a peculiar pendulum with a precarious pivot ?
A mistimed metronome???

Nay!

The old clock's clockworks wound up to *ticktock* by means
a bit more **deranged,**
as bells 3 and 4 tolled and the mechanism in question
hopped off its swing and ran away.

Dreadfully Dissonant and **tRauMaticaLLy** toned

clanked the **next three** of thirteen o'clock's chimes.
And with them

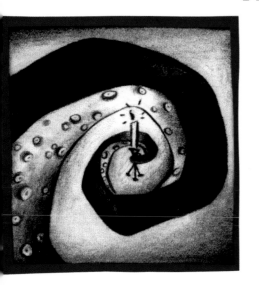

a slithery,

a spidery,

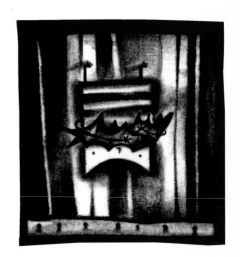

and a fluttery, leathery

all came looking for a place to *hide*.

The uncommon count of the old timer *continued*
as the 8th tremendously tedious toll tinged.
Then,
one after another
in a line front to back,
out floated four ghosts
with frightening groans
(in their stomachs)
who went straight to the kitchen
for a *mid-night snack*.

The next horrifying chime numbering 9
led to a curious clatter numbering 10,
the tenth tone to a horrendous number 11!
And with each haunting cue there came *another*
more horticulturally hideous than the other,
as a small pumpkin creep sister
and her creep pumpkin kid brother
were lent a lift to the ground by a ghoulish–
yet happily helpful—garden ladder!

Number twelve

"Number 12,"

chuckled one mischievous elf, as he danced a spooky jig with glee.
And then **there**, where any other clock
would have *naturally* stopped,
the weird ring-rackety
clock-oddity
did **not**,
as it tolled a   hollow and echoey,
and exceedingly   *eerie* number

13!

Just the tock-tick of the clock's click and the sound of night, that's all!

Sneaking sneakily...

creeping creepily...

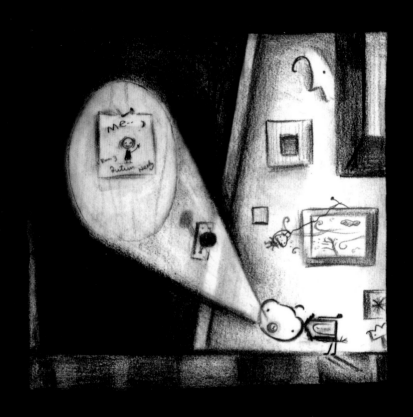

to the small girl's room at the end of the hall.

Open the door with a *squeeeeky* hinge,
it's time for mischievous things!
Sneaky, sneaky,
spooky and freaky,
on the count of (none other than) thirteen
the monsterous mischief begins!

"One"

"two"

"three"

"four"

"five"

"Six"

"seven"

"eight"

"nine"

"ten"

"eleven"

"twelve" . . .

chimed in an altogether
unexpected voice.
"Thirteen?!!?!"
shrieked a shocked chorus
of startled ghosts!
The bat, the bug, and the other ghouls

freaked

in disastrous *disarray*!
"Daunt!" "Haunt!" "Dismay!"
they squeaked.
"Run away!!!"
"Run away!!!!"

The mixed-up scene went from monsterous mayhem,
to a stop as *dead* as a graveyard lot.
When the ghoul crew realized that the uncanny culprit
behind the bewildering plot
was the prankster in pajamas, their small *friend*, not a fiend.
A miniature bewitcher with a devilishly silly double-dealing scheme!
Things were less *hex-ly* than they were hoax-ly!
More ridiculously girlie than they were *ghostly–*

and even the muddled monsters
found it all to have a fearfully funny ring.
For the small girl's *entirely* (if not at the very least mostly)
much too giggly for a gruesome ghastly,
and far too friendly for a frightful *anything!*

Late into the later late hours
they all played by the green moonlight,
as the winds howled outside
and the old house creaked.
It was a fairly normal night!
In a *fairly* normal house–that is,
if you're a ghost, a goblin, a beast, a bat, an it, or a thing...

or for that matter a small girl whose clock counts not twelve
but a spooky... kooky... *thirteen* !